I0689446

As Jaguars Dreamed On The Earth's Dark Face

As Jaguars Dreamed On The Earth's Dark Face

a magical realist novel in verse

Clif Mason

Cathexis Northwest Press

Endorsements for *As Jaguars Dreamed on the Earth's Dark Face*

Readers will be spellbound by Clif Mason's bold, courageous, and mesmerizing novel in verse, AS JAGUARS DREAMED ON THE EARTH'S DARK FACE. This visionary masterpiece depicts a world much like ours in which "No one claimed to want war / and yet everyone had a hand in it." Both an elegy for the *burning*, violence-ravaged earth and a praise song for the magnificence of its creatures, oceans, cosmos, and art, Mason follows two voices—a man's and his beloved's—as they communicate, while apart, through an ebony bead created by the woman. In language as marvelous as the tale being told, Mason never flinches from scenes of destruction in "the kingdom of flame / & annihilation." Neither does he cease from celebrating the power of the word-spells of poetry in which it becomes possible to participate in creation rather than destruction. In lines such as: "Every morning the rivers / forgot their names / so I gave them new ones" and "I didn't ask others / the nature of my task. / I simply sang threads of light / into night's dream ocean," this incantatory poem brilliantly reminds us of the holy, healing powers of art.

Judith Sornberger, author of *Sorority of Stillness: A Gallery of Women in Art* and *I Call to You from Time*

Clif Mason, soothsayer, oracle, cautionary tale-teller is our dream guide through this epic surreal poem "weaving" us into a Penelope-like tapestry of burning love. He sings with archetypal images so true we feel as though we've experienced all this before in our souls' cinematic journey (grief, despair, love, exaltation). Husband and wife, journeying separately, are accompanied by "a jet black bead." They search until they realize, "they were awake / when they dreamed" and "were now asleep" in this deathbed life review: "swirling drafts/ of kinetic,/ chaotic air . . . of spells filled with fire / & forbearance / fugues & fury." Echoing voices of Walt Whitman, William Blake and his angels, sounding akin to Edgar Allen Poe, the search continues through moons, suns, wars, human and animal emotions and experiences, "until the song was the blood / & the blood was the song . . . the beginning / & the end / of the beginning / of everything." Later, in Antarctica, the husband hangs the moon feather that drifts through the saga into his wife's hair. AS JAGUARS DREAMED ON THE EARTH'S DARK FACE should be read out loud with someone you love.

Barbara Schmitz, author of *Sundown at Faith Regional* and *Just Outside*

In this wide-ranging and dream-like poem, AS JAGUARS DREAMED ON THE EARTH'S DARK FACE, the speaker confronts the harsh realities of our world while on a quest to connect with love and beauty, with the goal of re-directing reality. War, violence, and deaths are expressed in surreal language. The diction is entrancing and images are striking, such as in "Trees galloped,/ a hundred horses, in the wind," and "Always the sound of water, the purl/ & purr of its flowing/ its carving and reaching," along with "We must count/ backwards,/ age after age,/ as wars batter the lands/ & their peoples,/ blasting into nothingness/ homes & stores,/ schools/ & hospitals,/ blasting bodies/ into rags/ & shreds." Like Odysseus, the protagonist experiences multiple trials along his journey; but ultimately, re-connection to love wins out. Mason is a seasoned wordsmith well worth traveling along with.

> Twyla M. Hansen, Nebraska State Poet 2013-2018, Author of *Inventions of Love* and *Feeding the Fire*

Clif Mason's AS JAGUARS DREAMED ON THE EARTH'S DARK FACE is a poetic journey that contemplates what it means to be human in the modern world. This evocative book of psalms—that balances hope and despair, peace and war, life and death—calls to mind the famous quote, "we're all just walking each other home." As the verses explore the natural and man-made, we must confront many harsh truths about our existence, but the magic of Mason's writing is that, once we embrace love, once we discover our true home, we are like the transformed protagonist finding, "Skin flushed with song,/ flesh sang with beat / & blood." This lovely voyage expertly crafted by Mason will be treasured and studied for years to come.

> Cat Dixon, author of *What Happens in Nebraska* and *Eva*

For Laurie, bead artist extraordinaire

Table of Contents

As Jaguars Dreamed on the Earth's Dark Face

and that love is a kelson of the creation
—Walt Whitman

Prologue

We lived in a time of war,
in which every door was blackened

with loss
& every street was electric
with angers & resentments.
Every home seethed
with unanswerable questions.
& at least one that wanted an answer:
What's to keep us from leaving

right now
& walking to Antarctica?
My beloved put down the cloth
on which she was sewing
a phantasmagoria of beads,
smiled & said,
Oh, maybe a few hundred miles
of cold ocean.
I hear it doesn't take kindly to foot traffic.
No,
we must each find our own way
to face down the darkness.
This is mine.
You lifted the round-
framed cloth,
painstakingly adorned,
hour after dreaming, patient hour,
with a splendor & a dazzle
of beads.
Sunlight struck,
seized,
& defined
each color, shape, & texture.

I could say nothing.

Go ahead, walk this long walk,
she said at last,
filling the air
with the words
of which I'd been incapable.
I'll give you, what,
a year?

I'll take a plane & wait for you
at the Amundsen-Scott Station.

Why don't you sail?
Shackleton's ship looked all wild
& weird
in the black-&-white photographs—
remember —
all frost-rimed,
its rigging hung with icicles,
as if festooned
for some winter solstice party.

They don't even make ships
like that anymore.
It's a plane or nothing for me.

We swam all night in the moon's golden lake
until,
at dawn,
we read from the book of waking,
every page luminous
& transparent.
Green light on morning's tongue,
a song sung
even in the shadows.
Trees galloped,
a hundred horses, in the wind.
Flowers lifted their heads,
& a thousand blackbirds
winged from the earth.

I didn't know the length of my journey,
didn't know if I'd end
the same person I'd begun.
But I trusted the red compass
of my blood,
& without another moment's worry
or hesitation,
I set out,
carrying my satchel of words
& new stars.

1. The Journey

1

As jaguars dreamed
on the earth's dark face,
the owl read
the book of night—
kenned its braille
as easily as someone
reads these lines—
& blue winds ghosted
around the trees.
Talons gripped the rabbit,
& blood burned in my body
like a star.
Daybreak spoke
her first green vowels,
& on all sides birdsong lifted
something resembling happiness
from the grass blades
to the highest boughs.

Sun emerged
& stunned every animate
& inanimate thing,
struck fire,
liquid, breathing flame—
from rocks & pebbles,
from cliff faces
& stone outcroppings,
from dust itself.

Molten rivers laid claim
to whatever was comforted
or contorted
by my name—
both the elements known
& those that would never be known.
To my surprise,
the sun didn't vaporize my face
or the consonants of my speech
or the craftiness of my fingers.
Instead,
she chose to preserve them—
like one of Herculaneum's intricate mosaics,
only alive.

2

        Hold this bead tight in your grasp,
my darling had said,
            taking it from a red silk pouch
                  & placing it in my hand.
        Say my name & I will be with you,
wherever you are on this earth.

        She'd fashioned the bead:
It was half as big as my thumb
           & black.
        Yet it had an endless array
of sparks within,
           like the night sky.

        I clasped the bead
              & she appeared.
        A star began to sing on my tongue,
& if we waited
          to learn the words,
              the song would be finished.
        Explosions on another continent
peeled skin from our flesh
           & glass slivers pierced our cheeks.
        Pain took apart everything,
             even poetry & art.

        Neither mountains nor stars
were permanent,
          just imponderably slow
            in their infidelity.

        The white water of longing
abraded our skin.

        When I stepped into her green chapel—
I felt shockwave
        & heat—
            as if lightning had struck
    ten steps off,
        ripping the air apart,
          stripping it of all but ozone.

        Stars were tattooed on night's skin,
& the moon shriveled like a leaf.

3

        The stillness of silk & silt.
        To what silence can I cling
that is salient in the night?
        Do I know the simple objects
                      of my daily walk,
     of my journey through trees
              & elusive clouds?
        How do I measure the vagaries
& variance
          of the real
            & unreal?

        Always the sound of water,
the purl
         & purr of its flowing,
             its carving & reaching.
        I heard it because it sought me out,
searched for the echo
        in my flesh,
           the movement in my blood.
        I heard it because it entered
& streamed through me,
         because it lit up my synapses
& lisped & lapped
           at every hidden cove & shore,
      at the long, unknown beaches within.

        Currents carried me to depths
yet unplumbed,
        so I might know more
          than fever dream or drama,
     pearl or peril.
        Waves washed away debts
& forgetfulness,
         doubts & regrets.
        They removed the deaths
            & dearths
       in which I conspired.

        When I was cleansed once more,
what acts would I own
        on the daybreak streets—
         with the slosh of water
       in my ears,

& in my mind
                                         the ceaseless,
                 unbroken cheer & chant
                             of the water vespers?

4

                    The day the war started—
                                         in countries
                     that were not my country—
the river flowed past
                                   in its calibrated banks.
                    The birds were noisy
                                 & then they were quiet.
                 Before,
death had been a matter of bodies
                             giving out over time, failing
of an instant,
                       of accidents,
                                    or of sudden hatreds
                    & blind blows.

             Now no death was unprecedented.
             No death was even unusual.
             Death had become
life's most common datum,
                       ordinary as greed,
                                    as the desire for revenge.

             No one claimed to want the war,
& yet everyone had a hand in it.
                 The killing & the dying
                                 became the rhythm of the day.

             Refugees streamed
                                 out of the hills & forests
                       & down the dusty roads.
                 They came all day & all night for weeks,
until there were millions in the camps.
                 There was no firewood
                                           & little food—
                     only what people carried.

             Cholera & dysentery
spread like rumors through the tents.

After a few weeks,
bands of men began to attack families.
They stole food
& beat the husbands
& held them at knifepoint
as they raped their wives & daughters
& mothers & sisters.
Afterwards, they cut everyone's throats,
even the children's,
even the infants'.

People saw their days darken,
& they knew what men did in the dark.

Husbands & wives still married,
children still found their way
into this world.
A few people wrote books,
& a few more read them.
Battles did not end the war,
but led only to other battles.
More & more land
was given over to graveyards.

The moon still rose,
the stars still appeared.
The sun still marched
without mercy
across the sky's battlefield.
The living didn't notice
& the dead didn't care.
The river flowed by,
the birds flew away—
leaving stray feathers
for poets & vagabonds to find.

The war went on.
Life went on—
& life had always been war.
Everyone said so.
It would still be war,
they said,
when the last of the midnight stars
blinked out.
No one doubted it,
not even children.

This was the way things were,
& the way things were,
they said,
was the way things would always be,
forever & ever,
without end.
Only the dead stars & poets
believed in peace.

5

I held the jet bead,
& my beloved was with me.
Her mouth was full of blue flowers,
my hands were cupped with rain.

We have this brief time, she said.

Walk with me, I said,
between the midwife's hands
& the summary executions,
between the first stars
& the last dreams.

Her arms were rivers
burning with reflected stars,
mine the aurora
reaching out in banners
of silk & milk,
streaming toward her
in coral-flaming heraldry,
carmine & green & golden.

Tell me a story,
she said,
of broken bodies
& forsaken delights.

Walk with me, I said,
between the pang & the pain,
between the sea's sultry
sighs & shrieks
& the forbidden sun's
gleams & glamor.

Her mouth was a new star

spilling silver into ebony night,
                             filling it with a luster of frost
        & opal & pearl.
         My eyes were dark unseen moons.

        What can we do,
                        she asked,
when falling stars
                 streak into the sea?

        Walk with me,
I said,
               & we'll learn the fever
      impelling us from this street to
                  as far away as Antarctica
& to the farthest star's
          incendiary heart.

6

        There was a horizon
beyond any horizon,
                  a depth beneath all depth.
       Questions questioned
                  questions,
      & answers hid in plain sight.
      I accepted this.
      Every place
was the center
             of every other place.

7

       In the humid air
of misty midnight,
                 I walked in disbelief
    through the dispossessed streets
          of a small town.
     Clouds lowered,
              dense as the oozy mud
     of a river bottom,
& throughout their massive,
          confused bulk,
they were infused with flame—
           no rusty ferrous sheen,
     no blush or flush,

but a blood-
red voracious fire.
This was no mellow glow,
as of half-
smothered embers,
but a deep ruddled burn,
a combusting flash
& shock-blast
of black smoke
& dark forest inferno—
a fulmination of scarlet-
raging cumulonimbus.
I felt scorched,
blistered,
cremated mid-step.

Did the townspeople writhe,
too, as they dreamed in sweat-
drenched sheets,
in sympathy
with my sudden pain?
Walking,
I felt a baleful heat
rolling out of that burning sky.
Neither sinless
nor particularly sinful,
I shuddered nonetheless
as the flaming angel passed by.

8

Every day
my head & my dreams
were filled with the war—
with the images
everyone had seen
on one screen
or another.
No one could escape them.
I could not escape them:
I saw them as the cameras
saw them,
heard them
as the microphones
heard them.

Cities' streets looked
                                    as if they'd been punched
& pummeled
                    by machines
                                        hundreds of feet tall,
            buildings like they'd been struck
                                by meteors.
            The fires could not be
                                            extinguished.
            They released noxious vapors
in the rolling plumes
                                of black smoke.

            I'd never seen so many ruined vehicles,
each bought with hours
                                    of someone's life.
            It no longer seemed a good trade.

            I passed blocks
of ransacked stores
                                        & wrecked office buildings.
            Warehouses looked like giants had used them
for footstools.
            Theaters were nothing
                                but hanging rafters,
                    smashed plaster,
                            & broken seats.
            The skyline that once looked
like money made visible,
                    now looked like a landscape
                                            of loss,
            a forest flattened by straight-
                                line winds.
            There were places
where neon still flickered,
                            places where water
                                        still jetted
                        from hydrants.
            Schoolyards were nothing
but mangled playground equipment.

            Backyards
                                    were filled with graves
marked only with stones
                        & pieces of rubble.

                    In some cases,
a name was scratched
                    into a broken piece of a door
                                        or a window
                    or coffee table.
            Empty lots had become
mass graves.

9

                    All I could do
                            in my vision
was avoid the outlaws
                    & outliers
                            & move as stealthily
as I could
                            through the cities of fragments
            & into the country.

10

                    In my mind,
I made the trip
                    from the prison camps,
                            before the cities burst
                    into cascading
incendiary explosions
                            & began to burn
            with such intense heat
                    the stones of the buildings
            & the ground itself melted,
                    as if they were being smelted
for new fashioning.
            What had been solid
                    was now loose,
                                        flowing,
                            molten rivers.
            They ran deeply over everything,
dissolving
            & evaporating it,
                                        destroying it
                    as if it had never been.
            The trip was extreme peril,
extreme fear,
                            extreme fire.

But, in my vision,
			I survived.

11

			Did I survive?
			It was hard to separate
						reality
from the hundred dream-
				sheaths of unreality.
			Once I had escaped
the kingdom of flame
						& annihilation,
				of seared flesh & burn scars,
I became soaked
			in the drench
					of freezing rain.
			Every muscle shuddered
& my teeth chattered
			so hard
					I thought they'd crack
			& fracture
in my mouth
			& I'd choke
				as I swallowed them.
			The freezing broke me
& I lost all sense
						of perspective,
				of direction,
					of up & down.
			I didn't know
if I was still on my feet,
				moving in a series of ever-
			more-weary spasms,
				or if I was lying prone
						somewhere,
afloat in a space
			that wasn't
				& couldn't be a place,
			if place meant
					or had ever meant
			anything of purpose or merit.

12

			In my vision,

the freezing was its own burning,
& I'd never felt so blazing,
blast-furnace hot.
I no longer knew
if I'd survived
the belching fire jets
of the burning camps,
or if I were in some coronal rapture
of final burning
that knew no end
& would never
ever flame out.
& then there was nothing:
no feeling,
no sensation at all,
neither within
nor without my body
or brain
or nervous system.
There was simply nothing,
no pain,
no quickening of the blood,
no sense of touch or smell
or taste
or hearing or sight.
All thought had become
so hopelessly knitted
& knotted,
so static
it was no longer a separate
pulse-firing of synapses,
no longer any kind
of movement,
not even
a mushy, sluggish one,
but a pathetic block
of what was not thought,
but what thought had once been—
the desecrated corpse of shadows,
of wraiths & smoke
& phantasms.
Time was not just incapacitated
or ended.
It was negated,
as if it had never been,
had never been dreamed

        or imagined.

13

        So, it wasn't in my life in time,
but in some wholly new irruption
                    into primal being,
      that whatever it was
    that I now was—
          & I had no idea
           what that was or might be—
began to be
       again,
           or perhaps for the first time,
     as if there had been no other.

      I couldn't tell.
      I was too raw,
too hollowed out,
          even to know when I began
to be deformed
       by desire,
            whether for the first
     or the ten thousandth time.

      & I began to perceive
or dream that I perceived
             our bodies,
     no longer burnt
        or frozen,
          but lying dazed
    yet open
         to the full dazzle
           of our senses,
    scattered through our bodies
         like stars through space.

      &, as stars congealed
        & concentered into whirling,
sparking
    spiral galaxies,
       my body became fleshed
             again,
     & all of the swift rivers
          of nerves
        stirred

& I began to smell
                & see & touch
                        & taste
                                & hear anew—
        or dream I did,
                        which was one & the same,
                as my dream was a body
& my body a dream.

                & I was shouting
                                        in joy,
                        & I was weeping,
        & before I even knew
                        I had stood up
                                        or how,
        I was dancing
                        & leaping
                & running for the pure bliss
                                of moving
        in my fresh-
                        wakened flesh.

                & I was singing—
what a surprise
                to be singing—
                                singing the song of my horrors
& sufferings,
                        singing of my escape
                                        & flight
        & of the sweet daybreak dream
                                of this new self.

                & my song was a promise:
Never again
                to betray & slay
                                        my best dream,
                my best hope
                        & desire.
        Never again.

14

                As I walked down that
                                        Texas blacktop,
I told myself:
        We must count backwards

                        to raise the dead
                of every war.
           We must help each other
                         keep the count.
           Time must be reversed
again
      & again.
          We must recite
                     backwards
          the prayers for the dead.

        Before our eyes,
we must see the wounds,
                  the injuries & killings,
           even as we speak the words
      that undo them,
              that instantly reassemble
        & rejoin
           the broken,
             the fragmented
        & destroyed.

        We must count
backwards,
          to reverse the unending
              flights of arrows
          slicing through bodies,
    & death's black winds
            blowing instantly in,
      spreading like ink
        through every vein.

        We must recite
backwards
        the prayers for the dead,
                    to reverse
         earth drinking gore
    as a leviathan drinks water.
     To reverse the screaming
of injured soldiers,
           who believe red ants
      are chewing
        through their chests.

        We must undo
the harvesting

of the fates' efficient shears,
as souls are cut
from the cloth of body
after body,
as the eyes of the dying
scan the ground
& see blood derangements,
shattered
& disarticulated bones,
death mold raging
through flesh
that swells like dried plums
dropped into water.

15

To end wars once
& for good,
we must reverse
the clouds of ash
that blow over the still living
& stick in their sweat—
slathering them
with mortality's funk.
We must,
through our words,
raise the dead,
who lie unburied,
decomposing,
dishonored.

We must,
by chanting backwards
the prayers for the dead,
restore the hopes,
scant or bountiful,
of those men & women,
of those children,
restore all the promise,
green or full ripe,
of their lives,
as those lives were the dark,
the irrecoverable,
costs of our hubris,
then,
as now.

16

          We must count
backwards,
              age after age,
                      as wars batter the lands
             & their peoples,
        blasting into nothingness
                  homes & stores,
             schools
                    & hospitals,
blasting bodies
           into rags
              & shreds.

          We must recite
backwards
                  the prayers for the dead
           that machine guns don't pulp
                thousands of bodies,
        leaving desolated armies
             & civilians
                  to row together
          into the clouds concealing
the immense river
           to the land of the dead.

          We must count
backwards.
         Bullets fly back into barrels
                    & artillery shells
          unconvulse.

          We must count
backwards,
         that sailors won't drown
                amid the wreckage
           of their ships,
that soldiers won't burn
                like rampaging stars
        or mortally wounded horses
                pant like spent lovers.

          We must recite
backwards
                  the prayers for the dead,

that ice won't form
around the moon,
that the circuitry of quietus
won't be recreated,
& that light won't burst
a million stones.

We must count
backwards
so the black swans of night don't fly
& the crows don't shake snow
from their feathers,
that the carrion dead
become carrion no more,
but rise—
so that they rise & live.

17

Released from my vision,
I walked into the moon's rondure
on the river's currents
& swam in a world of light.

The rushing water was cold
on my skin,
but I soon felt warm.
& I forgot all wars,
let them flow past,
liquid & formless,
without force
any longer
to maim or destroy,
or cut out my heart
or warp my dream
or garrote my hope.

I swam in the moon's light,
& its beams flowed
& flowered
on the dark currents.
Out of my hands swarmed
schools of Guadalupe bass
& white crappie.
I became a great catfish
swimming

             in that rippling light.

18

          Why did I walk there,
trudge through a land
              cracked & ravined
                        as a fractured skull?
          Why did I set one canvas-
shod foot in front of the other—
                      my own private death march—
        forsaken & fugitive,
              dream-curdled
          & futile?

          The answer was the single incandescent word:
Antarctica.
          Just to say it
              was to feel the burn
                of subzero air on my face.

          The land was so cold,
snow almost never fell.
          The continent,
                    once wed to India, Australia,
      & South America,
              was covered by more than a mile of ice.
          Its tallest mountain rose three miles.
          The South Pole itself
was ten thousand feet high.

          There was no mining,
              so the land was arsenic-&-zinc-
                        free,
nitrous oxide-free, hydrogen sulfide-
              free.

          It was a land without government.
          The emperor penguins
                  & orcas
did not wage war.
          Nor did the blue whales
                   & colossal squids.
          Even humans accepted it
as a Zone of Peace.

No limbs were severed there,
no bodies maimed.
No blood
was blown out of hearts,
no thoughts out of brains.

In the land of infinite whiteness,
of crisp starkness,
I sought the correcting of my vision,
the clarity of ice in my blood
& marrow.
& I sought love,
for I knew my beloved
would be waiting
at long journey's end,
with encircling arms
& a welcoming kiss.

For love.
I drank from my water bottle,
&, sweating,
set one determined foot
before the other.
For love.

19

The vast land of ice
was what I could imagine
but didn't yet know,
though imagining
was a form knowing took.
It was what I could feel
but didn't yet contain,
for such feeling could scarcely
be contained.

On my walk,
a dead rabbit kit
lay on its side in the grass,
its coat dusty & dry.
How few days it had had
to take in this wild world,
to make acquaintance
& find ways

to accommodate both pleasures
                              & risks,
                many, if not most,
                                        fatal.

              I was the fire
                        that burned up the world
as I perceived it—
                  ravenous as a tiger
                    for all things born of ardor
        & carbon.

              I was the fire that burnt up
the stars themselves,
                  insatiable,
                            feeding on their infinite
          hydrogen fusions.

              That was the day I defied
& banished forever
                        every spiteful self-
                                        torture
                        & distress.
                  No more cuts
of the knife
                        of those confusions.
              I refused to bleed out
                              irascible doubts,
delusions of gravity
                  & grandeur.
              I burned up all knives
                        & the kindred of knives.

              I burned
& consorted
                        with others who burned—
each an inferno.
              Unafraid,
                        I called this burning
        by its true name,
                              love,
              yes,
                  simply love.

20

       I found this feather on my walk.
       Perhaps it would fit
another's wing.

       Blue streets in the evening light.
       Lamps were burning in every home.

       Yesterday's hail had ravaged flowers,
stripped petals
                    & driven them into the dirt,
    had filled the yards
          with leafy twigs.

       Not one of the hailstones remained,
yet their damage was everywhere.
       What I saw was the record
of a small battle,
         in an obscure war
           the world was having with itself.
       There were no survivors
in this war.
       In time,
             everything
               & everyone
       would be slain.

       That evening was so still
& the streets so blue.
       This was not war,
             but peace.
       I greeted a man on the sidewalk
but he hastened
           into the shadows.
       The cars on the street
had turned to rust overnight.
       A good wind would scatter them
             like dust.
       The light poles suffered
from a chronic calcium deficiency.
       They shrank another foot each year.
       Red-headed woodpeckers were at work
on the houses.
       One day someone would turn
             down this street

& see nothing but plumbing
             protruding from the foundations.
       When someone asked about a neighbor,
a friend said,
       He went to the store
                   to buy some milk & eggs.
       I thought he'd be back by now.
       No one says what really happened:
He sprouted wings
                   & flew off like a condor,
       dead set on reaching the horizon
                   before sunset.
       That had been months ago.
       He wasn't answering his phone,
& his property taxes
                   were overdue.
       At some point,
someone would pay what he owed
                   & claim his property.
       I reckoned that's what life was,
one person after another
                   losing their purchase on the earth
       and others benefitting from their loss.
       The sooner one got used to it,
the happier one might be.

21

       Way late & waylaid.
       The day was so splendid,
I wandered for hours
             down paths fringed
                   by wide swaths of wildflowers.
       This was what body & breath,
muscle & mind,
                   were for.
       This was what time's
language improvisations
                   were for.

       I heard the crying of the beets,
deeply entombed in soil.
       The cucumbers were sympathetic,
                   making their homes in air,
             like birds,
but they realized there was little

              they could do.
      Others were buried alive,
          as well—
carrots, potatoes, & onions;
        kohlrabi, radishes, & rutabagas;
    horseradish & yams.

      What did one life know of another?
      What window could one look through?
      Was there some celestial cable
that could link
          my love's gravity to mine,
    some line of words that ran direct
          from my mind to hers,
     some verbal black bead?

      Every day new words
sought me.
      I'd considered searching
for the words,
         but whenever I'd done so,
    I'd found only 3D-printed copies.
     They couldn't do any of the things
real words did.

      So I waited for the words
          to surprise me.
      What did I want from the night
of white-barked trees,
         of frog-throated rivers?
      How many dreams did it take
to fill the great lake of this life,
         to kill the stories that kept me
    from quenching my thirst?
      What did I want
from the smoldering moon
          of my yearning,
    the ocean of desire
        so dark & wide
    no ship could ever cross over?
     Time was born again & again—
from the leaping of fish
         & leopards,
    the diving of hawks
      & humpback whales,
the running of wild horses

                              & cheetahs.
               It was up to me not to betray
their trust.
               It was up to me
                     to burn,
         in that time born,
                  in words.

22

               A cabal of stones slid down the street
& rendezvoused
                             in a park after midnight.
               The unearthly work of healing
their backyards' blighted,
                  misbegotten hopes
                                   began:
               What would they do
to inspire the desperate?
               What platform of charms
                     would they champion
         without question?
               They were each accountable
for the integrity
                  & discipline of their work,
                     for their allegiance
          to any & all future acts.

               Together they edited
                  their declaration of challenges,
their articles of unfathomed faith.
               They submitted the detailed documents
of reproaches withheld
                     but not forgotten.

               They levied pledges
& promises,
                       & together they fashioned
         a singular authority
                 none could assume on their own.
               Together they resolved
to own the nights of sleeplessness
                     & fasting,
         the persistent rites
               of the shaping of breath.

Derangement & atrophy
          were everywhere.
The metamorphosis of apathy
was never complete.
Each must declare their comfort
with doubt,
    own their hesitancy
        to enhance their choices.
Each must canonize
    the daybreak
they might not live to see.

23

The anger of roses,
the pity of apricots.
    I couldn't trust
        the world to make sense
any more than I could trust
    the ocean not to ransack the land.
There were no longer
any harmless thoughts.
Everything lethal betrayed me,
& everything might someday
        become lethal.

The person who loved salamanders
& chameleons
    might go screaming
        down an alligator's gullet.
The person who delighted
in feeding the geese
        might waken in the grip
of a grizzly's claws.
What sacrifices did my fellow citizens
make to the gods of airplanes
        & roundabouts?
Who stepped forward
    at the carnival
to become the first human
    catapulted into Earth orbit?

As requested,
I recited the ten thousand names
    of the griefs that populated
the streets of my city's brain.

I'd probably never know
                              if it worked or not.
            I didn't feel different,
any less sorrowful.
            That didn't mean
                        I wasn't different.
            Perhaps that was one more
in a chain of invisible changes
                              that would, at some point,
      add up to a significant change,
one that *was* visible.
            Perhaps this wasn't a change at all.
            No star had left its galaxy,
no moon had slipped its orbit.
            My life remained what I made of it,
until perhaps
                              ten thousand tomorrows from now,
      I'd know if I'd truly lived
                        the life given me.

24

            Bodies would break
before they could break down
                              the savage proteins
of one's propensities.
            Stomach's hydrochloric
                        could not digest them.
            What charming other choices
were the stinging insistence
                        of spring rains,
      the gentility & grace
                              of tree frogs.
            Who could help but be enamored
of the herbivorous efficiency
                        of walking sticks,
      the repartee of roosting turkeys,
                  the insouciance of marigolds & coyotes?

            Each of us had our partialities
& proclivities.
            Knowing them was the first step
                        to undoing them.

            I might learn to prefer,
after all,

                    the raucous, no-holds-
                              barred candor
                                        of a murder of crows.

25

                    When the sun's code was broken
          & all the daylight
                              emerged at once from the chest
          in which someone had carefully laid
                                        the stars,
               when lightning ignored the trees
                              & windmills & electric poles
                    & went looking for a person,
          any person,
                              but especially the one summoned
               from the dark barn
                              by midnight's stony rapture,
                    who chose to stand alone
                              in a pasture,
          when the calendar sneezed
                              & all the days
                              fell out of the next year,
          when a moratorium was declared
                              on all plans for the rewiring
               of past premonitions
                              & future dreams,
          the beacon at a small-town airport
                              scoped the hearts of clouds
                              without fail,
               & I offered a hundred years
                              of found feathers
          to the winds that returned daily
                              to reclaim my blood
               & the names I spoke like prayers
                              to the night
               & to the dawn.
26

                    My body grew tired
          from carrying me along—
                              all my weight of grief
               & of a gladsomeness so protracted
                              it seemed innate.
               I'd not been given the name
                              of *anxious.*

It wasn't in my collection of names.
But *sanguine* was,

                          & *merry.*

        I wasn't sure
where I'd picked them up,

                or when.

        How many changes

                   must a person make?
        My whole life had been
one continual chrysalis.
        I knew I must cut through

                  the sheer veil again
    & push through,

             become something else,
       become some*one* else.

27

        In my hand a bead,
& in that bead

                  the blackness of space
      opened.
     When the city was indentured

               to time & fear,
we were freakish as feldspar,

        as Greek spearmint—
   a smell like green smoke,
        fearless & eerie

            in the mouth,
    & lingering,

      lingering.

     She wanted boundless pastures
of will & gold.
     I wanted submarine shores

           of marl & rose.
    Her tongue
was a chalice,

      my shoulder,
        bare star
         become barren harrow
     of bone,
  become errant morning,

       brash rain.

She wanted the blind flame
of the total solar eclipse.
I wanted the music
of mirrors & magnesium.

We flamed,
acetylene,
in an ice-
locked lake,
melted it
with molten muscle
& blood.
We galloped on horses strong
& fleet
across fields flat
as tambourines.

She opened her eyes
& I felt star
-burn.

Afternoon grew obsidian walls
& chill held the trees
in amorous arms.
We turned to the room
of heartbeat & jewel.

We kissed.

The bedposts kindled.

II. The Bead Artist at Break of Day

28

         In my beloved's long absence,
his long passage across land
            & ocean,
                  I waggish wandered
in clouds & forests,
          feathered & ferned,
                ferried
          from the time
disease's winter winds
               frosted the cheeks
        of so many—
cheeks now cold
          as the last words
              of lost love—
     & I was, in their wake,
            awash in unwonted sentiments
(salt-&-silica-
        silted sediments),
   ferried to my own place,
                  unique
           & oneiric,
      of unceasing dearness
        & delight.

       I beaded a vast collective dream,
a spell that resisted
             & altered
     reality altogether.
    When the world
         showed itself apocalypse
     & apocrypha,
& the kitchen machines
           abruptly stopped,
    did I open or close
   the book of daybreak?
   Did straws shiver
        on the broom at night?

29

      Sometimes it was all I could do
to forgive the world,
      forgive & forgo
          & let my *No*
    define me.

What did the orphaned moon
say to the planet of fire,
                              the planet to the invincible star?
Daybreak burned in the cold,
& song—
                spell of all spells—
                                became the world.

My heart cried out
like a barred owl.
                I listened
                        & followed it
                                    all the way
        to daybreak,
                    to a renewed love
                                of time—
                    as embodied,
                as felt,
                        as it might become.

For me,
each daybreak
                                was elegy
        of the day before,
                                    hymn
                to the day to come.

30

                In a time half-
created by fable & fear,
                    starveling winds
                                filled my ears
        with the stars' darkest secrets,
& the moon's fractured light
                                burned clouds
                unable to flee.
        Cumulus bled maroon
                                    & dusky rose.
            Schooled in light,
scarified by rain,
                    I walked invisible
                                as a shadow at night,
        as a flame in the pyre
                    of noon.

31

What did the daylily tell of hawks
& hapless mice,

or of the brainpans
of stars breaking all day?

When the world was laced
with arsenic & randomness,

repugnance & lies,
who could say how deep
into dawn
the snowy owl's cry
resounded

or how night music
might become daylight chant,
& dread

prayer?

32

The sleep of the music,
dreaming,

silent,

in the piano's black coffin.

The sleep of the bridles,
hung,

a dozen cautionary tales,

on the barn wall.

The long-necked amphorae,
confident goddesses
of the wedding party that never was.

The sleep of the plane,
waiting patiently in the dark hangar
for the double doors to slide open
on the day it would land,

pinwheeling
down a runway,
shedding horror at every turn.

A movie theater in which the film
of my lost days played,

perfect memories,

                                on a continuous loop.

        When time & remembrance
were a dream of clouds,
                incensed amethyst-
                                jasper,
        frozen obsidian-
                maroon,
                        I became a lover of clouds
& I knew I was at earth's mercy.

        When remembrance & time
were a dream of clouds,
                roiling amethyst-
                                silver,
        I gave myself
                        to a different dream,
defying time
                & defining a world
                        not yet charted
                or conceived.
        I released the hunting leopards
of my new ambitions.
                I inspirited the nightingale singers
                        of my passions,
        quickened the spiraling otters
                of my yearnings.

        Lightning wrote its magnesium script
across memory's midnight sky,
                                & I asked,
        *What dreams unsettle
night's unholy crypt?*
        *What light makes night
                take off its frozen mask?*

        I was taking a long walk
when I turned
                        & walked straight out
        of my body.
        Words & forms
took shape in my mind.
        I knew that,
                        after my vanishing,
my bead paintings
                might remain,

        like dew on grass,
             like memory.

33

      Soft bituminous night
in the country of dreams,
            & the stars were brash as dust
     thrown in my eyes.
      In the moon of birthing horses,
         all the foals followed their mothers,
mad for the milk
       they'd turn into galloping hooves.
     Feral cats stole into the night,
         in pursuit of their meat,
& swans floated like paper boats.
     In the morning,
          the sleep masks
       all fell away.
     Some had no faces:
They were like windows.
     Everyone walked around,
         dressed in their losses.

34

     Every morning the rivers
         forgot their names,
so I gave them new ones,
        names of sleek,
    sibilant sounds.
   The rain chanted the names,
& the daybreak birds
          celebrated them from all sides,
     until the stones hummed
   & the daylily
      & carnation petals
        whispered them.

35

     I was a creature made for joy,
though the world
     continually delivered
       the mail of sadness
    to my door.

I levitated
around the neighborhood,
talking to myself,
muttering the words
of invisibility
& suspending
the law of gravity.
I heard dance music
from the country
of childhood.
On the street,
desperate men sold knives
made of blue air.
No one knew
they'd been cut
until they collapsed
with a shirt full of blood.

36

What did I say in my dreams—
standing beneath a cadmium comet,
facing the buffets
of a phosphorus wind?
Did I choose
to sing the ballads
of the inconsolable,
heat-stroked with loss,
or to chant
good luck charms
for the destitute?
Or did I go further
& enspell the air—
fill the sky with waterspouts
& floating labyrinths?
I didn't ask others
the nature of my task.
I simply sang
threads of light
into night's dream ocean,
silent fins
dividing dark waves.
I sang until my fingers
turned to glass
& shimmered
when I held them up

to moonlight.

I beat unknown rhythms
on the tympani of verbs
& let the trumpets of nouns
announce themselves
& parade through scales.

Words became the mongoose that seized
the cobra,
the wolverine that stood down
the polar bear.

37

Shadows lit
the moon's dark side,
& stars spread their black dreams
across night's bright water.
The trees were anthracite
& their roots green.
Their boughs were made of mercury.

The stars walked on islands
of black glass.
Light was suspended
from a paralytic moon.

Hundreds of crystalline birds
hid in the machines
of treetops,
& they sang in the language
of secret names.

Few things were as sacred
as the question,
as deserving of reverence.
Though I might try,
I could not tear the fabric
of the question.

What would happen
if the winged horse
of the question were slain—
murdered
by a spear of rose petals?

The questions were secret names,
were migrations
on which we could carry nothing,
neither provisions
nor changes of clothes.
The names remained
their own intense discipline.
They taught me
what they wished to say,
& they give me those things—
& nothing more.

No stars could chart our travels
& travails.
Every arrival
was a departure.
I burned
off the morning mist,
& when I did,
I found the sun of questions
had risen,
the sum
of secret names.
& everywhere
there was daybreak
& the waking
from forsaken dreams.

38

Holding a jet black bead:
Five spells on my lips
became five rivers
in my mind.
Five rivers became
five lanterns in my heart.
Five lanterns became
five rooms in my dreams.
Five rooms became
five lions
stalking memory's savannahs.
Five lions
became five spells
on my lips.

39

        Between the spine of glass
& the face of twigs,
                        the green veil
          & the sleeping violin,
    night smothered day
             beneath its black pillow.

        Constellations rose,
                hoarfrost
      on jet sky,
& two humpback whales slept,
                 vertical tails
    a foot off the ocean floor—
        galleons looming
            in black fathoms.

        Some days I wailed & wept,
like the moon with broken ribs,
                or I sang,
    like the desert dreaming it was a sea.
    I taught my song
          to a morning glory,
& then there were two of us
            to weep & sing.

        Between the broken candle
& the silk curtains,
      the gold leaf
            & the galloping horse,
    I read from the diary
of barred owl nights
      & poems took flight,
         commanding the air.
    I dreamed the world around me,
wove it like a cloak of leaves.
    Did the moon,
        conversant in many languages,
    intercede for me
          with the wind?
    Words questioned
        their ordinary meanings
& deserted the dictionary
      of portents.

I was not a floating dandelion seed.
No,
                              I was a great blue heron,
migrating undaunted,
                         against even the most punishing
             winds.

40

             Stillness still unstill.
Wind whistling,
                                   whirling through dust.
             I was here to illumine shadows,
not hide in them,
                   to break day,
                            not cleave to night.
             Just so
did I change
                   to chant mourning's new morning
                              & jubilation song—
as earth's wildling chorus
                   sang its freshest tune.

             I no longer gave ear
to winter's sober cobalt dirge,
                            no longer felt its dull-tolling,
             sorrowful bells,
                   downcast & lasting
                              & sonorous & slow,
rolling out one long lone bone-
                   crushing tone of numb dumbness
             & melancholy—
                            but sang praise anthems,
sang of grass' green crossbow bolts
                            shot from soil,
             of clouds in irradiant boil.

41

             What ardent color
was the army of my will,
                   the spill & shill
                            of those irrepressible vernal,
near-supernal songs,
                            the long-delayed,
             voicings

      & rejoicings of my stylings,
    perhaps inimitable,
          perhaps ineluctable?

    I breathed & my blood brightened
& my mouth bloomed,
        an iris in a garden of faces.

    Did I ride the white-water engine
over rocks & stumps,
     & drink from stalactites
        in a cavern's heart?

    I burned in the moment
until my lamp glowed from the enkindled oil,
       gleamed like glass as it melted
   & returned to the shore
        on which I stood,
    singing.

    & the song swept out
from the words on a torn scrap of paper,
     & my blood raced with the song,
   flaming as it flowed,
       until the song was the blood
    & the blood was the song,
      flaming as it raced
from the land
     to the stars
       to the single point
    that was the song
& the blood,
    the beginning
       & the end
  of the beginning
    of everything.

42

    I dreamed continually
       of metamorphosis,
of things becoming
     other things—
  hummingbird & hawk,
 ocelot & sea otter,
    topaz & amethyst.

I spent hours watching the changes
of bodies & flames,
    & I understood:
        Bodies *were* flames.

43

    Skin of ice, skein of yarn,
scone on saucer.
     None was content being itself.
     Each wanted to become a metaphor,
        any figure of speech.

    The water in the kitchen sink
secretly yearned to become Lake Superior,
        Lago Titicaca,
    or even the Amazon,
   a river so immense
      no one would ever dare dam it up.

    The Pacific pondered,
in thoughts deep
       as the Mariana Trench,
   what it would mean
    to become a continent,
      an island,
    a simple garden plot,
     a grave.

    That day all aphorisms
turned to golden dust
       & dispersed.
    The long-necked cranes
     of epic poems
      forsook their shelves
& flew off to nesting grounds
     deep in the summery north.
    Millions of lyric butterflies
      winged from books
   & flitted across deserts & plains
     & high up
      & over
    hills & mountains.

44

I composed my daybreak letter,
written to no one,
                                        not even myself.

             Did I yearn to become consequential—
in some way necessary
                as sunlight or water,
                        as the seeds that grew
to become new entrancements
                                on our tongues,
        the fruits of our thoughts
                & labor?

             When I prayed in the green cathedrals
of the cucumber,
                when I prostrated myself
                        in the red mosques
                of the pomegranate,
when I sang a cappella
                        in the yellow temples
                                of the starfruit,
        I learned again that sweetest
of sweet communions:
                                the drawing
        & releasing of breath.

             Did I crave a life
that was the daily work
                of my love,
                        a love so vast & riverine,
        so mysterious,
                I could not help but set it down in a letter,
so,
        come the first hard frost,
                        I might know something
                beyond impermanence,
                        beyond metaphor,
something that would live
                even as we disappeared,
                        keep making its movies
        even as we slept,
                whether that be for one time
                        or all time?

             The remarkable
might still make its home

                                        in my best self.
              I might yet become
                        the minister of the possible,
  & the remarkable
                        might yet become
                                but one thing I trafficked in.

              Daybreak flaming through amethyst
                                        made mercy,
        & mercy made change,
                        possible.

45

              I lay sleeping,
                                a seed in rich soil.
              After a spring storm,
  my roots pulled themselves arm-
                        over-arm
                                down through
                wet loam & seized hold.

              & I uncurled—
  lithe dancer—
                        unfurled myself
                                into eager tendrils,
        wild & green
                        & burning to flower.

              I studied the alchemy
  of forsaken time.
              I heard the music,
                                felt the mystique,
                        of snow,
  the radiant cadence
                        of wind in the branches,
        feathers kissing air.

              The moon was dust & rock
  made splendid by sunlight,
                                a pock-marked face made holy
            beyond all hope
                        or dream of home.
          Seeing it,
                I heard the vast song
                                sung under

& behind
         all the songs
                  I'd found my way to sing.

                  The moon burned
                           through its battered face,
my lips parted,
                  & a free tongue intoned
                                    the strangest,
most surprising of chants,
                  the unchanging one
                                    that I,
         among the most changeable
                           of changeable creatures,
                  was never taught,
                  but was born,
                                    nonetheless,
                  to sing.

                  I lingered in cascades
of clouds & sounds,
                  one dream displacing another,
                                    replacing it
         with a new dream,
                           jetting through blood & mind
                  kinetic,
                                    intimate.
                  World & time
were vast
                                    & past intricate.
                  I became aware
                           of the recreating
         of the secret fabric of things—
no,
                  not so much a recreating
                           as a re-plaiting—

                  when I spoke a name,
                  when I intoned
                           the holy nomenclature
         of first things,
                           princely & proud
                  or unabashed
                           in their bashfulness:
                  the bending,
                           the repairing of the rupture,

the re-binding—
perhaps rapture too—
to be made whole
through a new enlacing.

The name healed a space
in which I could discern
all the carbon
& non-carbon forms
light embraces & awakens,
adores & adorns,
all the crystal particles of wind
& air & water vapor,
all the seeds & shades
of meaning & defining,
nearness & care,
in spite
of whatever else I might feel
whatever else I might know,
islands hinting
at the mainland lying beyond,
over that water,
behind those immense clouds—
when I spoke a name.

46

I was an ingot
of rain.
I was a waterfall
of invisible ravens.
I was a mirror
of burning jaguars.
I was a comet
of frozen spells.
I was an ebony bead,
veined with burning prayers.
I was a firefly chorus,
flashing
binary code.
I was a snowy owl,
gliding
on currents of moonlight.
I was a glacier
of radiant dreams.
I was a mouth

of nitrogen
                                        & fire.

47

                    I addressed the great horned owl:
                        The raging moon
makes an inferno
                                        of the sky's black waters,
            & you swim
                        in burning oceans of light.

                    Think now of this long-dead dream
of the sugar-blooming,
                                            all-consuming moon,
                the ruin & wreck
                            of its trajectory
                                after the planet-
                    smashing,
                                        feral,
            ignorant punch
& concussion
                        that thrust out
                                one immense fragment,
            to spin
                        in earless, airless dark,
afflicted for ages
                        beyond ages
                                    by some species
                    of cosmic delirium tremens,
            until it slowly grew tranquil,
                            sitting space zazen,
                    floating
                                in its lavish robe
                        of dust
            & dressed
                        in black rock
                            & desolation:
                                an orphaned child,
                    a grave of gravity.
                Think now of its quiet,
                                    insistent summons—
how it draws
                        these five low emphatic notes,
                                nasal flute song,
            from your throat & beak,

just as it draws
the answering call,
differently pitched,
from your mate,
& just as it draws
these words
from my mind,
how it tightens your talons
on the frozen-
brittle
skeletal branch
of the hundred-year-old pin oak
& torches the forest floor
your yellow eyes
scan for merest movement.

You descend,
gliding in silence
through ice-white
burning shafts
of raging lunar light.

48

I held the black bead
& he was with me:
During the brightest full moon
in 133 years,
the crabapple tree in our yard
cast long shadows,
thin as spider legs,
on snowy earth,
& our naked eyes
could scarcely make out
the huge lunar maria.
They were filled
with white light,
as if,
volcanic,
it had flowed up
& burst from lunar mountains,
plunging out,
roiling in firestorm,
& lunging into depressions
in driving, irradiant rivers
& waves.

We lay on our backs
                on the snowy driveway
to steady the binoculars,
        & our eyes smarted,
     as if we'd looked
             straight into the noonday sun
       as it touched its torch
          to a snowbank—
      yes,
a retina-searing cascade
       of sparks.

      Maria & craters' names
         were blessings,
             charms:
     Mare Tranquillitatis,
        Mare Serenitatis,
           Tycho.
     Snow in the yard
         burned with moon dazzle,
blazed around us
      like the light-deluged moon.

49

     Dreamwalking, I saw him.

     All day,
shadows moved
         in the fields beside him
    & behind him
      on the road he'd chosen.
     When he was thinking
about something else,
        the shadows rose
         & broke
      into storms of blackbirds.
     He didn't run
or drop to the ground
        in fright.
     He didn't turn
& flee
      the way he'd come.
     He trusted his sense of direction,
        trusted his road
      was the right road.

                    He began to sing
& the words became
                                        his torch.
                    He began to sing
                                        & the winged ones
                        stopped flying.
                    The blackbirds
became shadows.
                    Green moss lay
                                        its bright robe
                        over the forest floor.
                    If he failed,
he'd fail
                                    as this moss failed,
                splendid.

50

                    Every night I dreamed of ocean.

                    Did my love seek coral burial,
bereavement in shadow-
                    dust & smoke-vapor
                                        coalescences of mist
        & blood—
                    ocean,
                        because ocean could be
                                            a space
                    outside of space
                                        to rest.
                    Immovable,
immeasurable,
                    it was cold & rolling,
                                        aging,
                                            raving
            against everything
                        dear & dire that chose
                                    to lay itself down
                in sacrifice or service.

                    The wildling sea
was not the bewildered dream
                                        perhaps he thought it was,
            but the surging burn of moon.

                    Yearning thwarted,

                                    he did not spurn
what could not be felt or known
                    in the typhoon & trance
                                his dancing voice requested—
            as he trained ear & eye
                                    ever more insistently
                on what was far too blue-blue-blue
                                        baroque
                    to be blathered,
                                too bellicose
to be hallucinated or hoped,
                    not matter how spirit-altering
                                    his purpose.

            Did sea walls hold firm
against the battering arms
                    & shoulders
                                    of the stone-
                        shattering waves?
            Did the phantoms melt
                    & flow,
                            like immolations,
or did day forget itself
                    & let radiance burn
                                through the cracks & fissures
in the world as he imagined it,
                    as, for one short moment,
                        everything became luster
        on water,
                light upon light
                                    upon light,
        & he knew once more
                    he could blaze
                                in the wild flame
            at the wild core of words?

51

            Every night I dreamed of ocean.

            I cupped hands
                                        to catch rain
falling straight from the moon.
                My hair & clothes were soaked,
                            & I wanted never
                to be dry again.

I was river & ocean
the book of waters,
whose pages
never stopped turning.

As the sea's green horses
galloped against the land,
froth-maned,
snorting,
& stamping,
their eyes became
black storm,
their teeth pale lightning.

They whinnied & neighed,
turned on sharp-
planted hooves,
loped down sandy strand,
& plunged
to their withers.

Immersed,
they swam into the breakers,
until their green dissolved
in green
& they were lost
in darkness.

The horses left behind
only moonspells,
in which,
saturated by salt,
sea spray & splash,
they were taken off their feet,
dunked,
stunned,
& spun,
grasped by resistless
tidal force.

The undertow of words
gripped them,
drew them deeper,
deeper down—
but they did not drown.
Instead,

they grew sharp red gills,
                    learned new breathing,
                              became mermaids,
        & spoke these words:
            Let us stretch taut
                this nautical line of vowels,
                          tie down this rigging
                of slant-rhyming ropes.
            Let us unfurl sails
to billow with the breezes,
                & fly
                        to some unseen land,
          some island not in ocean at all
                        but in the vast
            cosmic spinning.

52

            What would happen
                  if I beaded daybreak's words
                onto silk?
          I sang in beads
a dream tale
                of reckless hunger
                      & angry ghosts,
          of the moon of my love
                      sown like a seed
              in the soil of dreams,
of unbroken horses
                galloping
                    through black conflagrations
        in unchanging night,
          galloping toward a land of ice.

          In beads,
I sang of swirling drafts
                of kinetic,
                    chaotic air,
           of spells filled with fire
        & forbearance,
                fugues & fury.

          I sang for hours,
chanted spells
                in the dream cavern
                        as I beaded.

Under a moon
of crematory dust,
assaulted by the rust
of baroque incursions,
sanctioned unsanctionable abuses,
I wrote in beads
in the book of daybreak.

53

In the country of dreams,
friends asked me to say more,
but I wondered what more
I might rightly say
about the fabulous indulgence
of finches,
little thimbles of the goddess,
or the extravagance
of maple samaras—
gold helicopters
cruising the neighborhood
like minuscule news crews.

A twig released a hummingbird,
& I abandoned fear
& leapt
onto a running bison's back.
Or I lived in air,
a dragonfly speeding,
a living string of beads,
through cattails,
a red-tailed hawk
claiming more clouds
with every wingbeat.
Or I was a wolverine—
a grizzly squeezed
into the skin of a marten—
made to defy
with every fiber
of nerve & long claws.

54

What could I say
after so many words,
so many spells?

Plant trees & poems,
hardiest of perennials.
Always face bracing winds,
kiss warm lips.
Every moment is a flower
& a star,
& this life
both a garden
& a galaxy.
A great deal can yet be done
if you put your whole spirit
& body to the task.

As the poem was spoken,
its lines disappeared into air,
word by word,
syllable by syllable.
Its spell had begun.
It entered the world
& became the world.
& the world became
the poem.

III. Antarctica

55

                 & then the women were gone.

                 A plowshare dredged
a girl's groin,
                             & a red star crushed her windpipe.
                 Her brain smoked
like liquid nitrogen,
                     & she struggled
                                 in a delirium of ghosts
         & forgotten time
                     to rise.
                 Her eyes were meteors
                                     burning up
                 in the night sky.
                 She sutured her own mouth shut
with black thread
                                 & wasted,
                 waned like the bulimic moon.

                 The old woman
                                 said she still saw her
                 in Juárez,
a single star,
                 floating in infinite blackness.

56

                 Inside the ant's cathedral,
night exhaled a rose
                 of stars & iron,
                                 of helium & salt.
                 There was no
                                 forgiveness.
                 Everyone's feet were nailed
to the stone
                             of time's indifference.

                 Rapists' fingerprints
                                 grew gray spiders
             & knife blades.
                 Their foreheads dripped
sweat & steel springs,
                     lizards & stunted trees.

Morning's light was thin
& burnt out,
with an undreamt of pallor,
& air quivered with heat.
It shrank the skins of tarantulas
& made the cactus thorns
brittle,
dryly brutal,
complicit in the wind-
blown murders
of moths & small birds.
People's shadows bled
scorpion tails,
hawk beaks,
& rattlesnake scales.

57

The city
was no longer a city,
but a morgue.
Death was the green bird
flying from house to house
& in each home
a mother died
or a daughter died;
a sister died
or a wife died.

The bird sang
& a hundred women
fell dead at once.
It sang
& the cemeteries
sprang up.
It sang
& the living
wept inconsolably,
smeared ashes
on their faces.

The green bird flew in
& out
of houses & churches,
of stores & factories.
The bird flew faster

& no one could catch it.

              The women
                              continued to fall.

              They fell in the night
& in the day.

              The women
                              continued to fall.

58

              Wine drops drove
                              claw hammers,
through the foreheads
                   of derelicts.
              Five suns
burned out
                   in my hand.

              Plant managers
drained workers' blood
              & transfused them
                   with diesel fuel.
              I wanted to save them
but could not.

              Bored store clerks
                   pushed syringes of blue stars
         into their veins.
              Black stones
fell from my mouth.

              Someone dismembered
a boy
                              & left his heart
              in the parking garage.
              Five suns
                   burned out
         in my hand.

              A crowd of strangers
surrounded me,
              their minds full
                   of rusting razor blades.

                    I wanted to save them
but could not.

                    Skeletons sat
                                        in echoing houses
& beat each other
                        with wrist bones
                                                & femurs.
                    Black stones
fell from my mouth.

                    We carried dead children
                                        through our days.
                    They lay in state
in our brains'
                                        crystal coffins.
                    Five suns
burned out
                                        in my hand.

                    A black moon
drank black constellations
                                        from a black sky.
                    I wanted to save them
but could not.

                    People woke,
                                        rinsed faces
                with dead engine oil.
                    Blood blisters
bloomed
                                        like smallpox spots.
                    Black stones
fell from my mouth.

                    Five suns
                                        burned out
                in my hand
                    I wanted to save them
but could not.
                    Black stones
                                                fell
                        from my mouth.

In my grasp,
the bead
                    that was night itself.

My love kissed
the black pearls
                    of my eyes.
I touched gold moonlight
                    on her neck.

We talked
& our children
            were adopted,
                    born anew,
                        & fostered
            into our family—
snuggling against us,
                    blind as newborn otters.

We talked
& night bled
                    indigo,
                        apricot,
            blood rose—
                    the colors of her bead paintings.
            & when we were silent,
my words were inked
                    on air's transparent page.

I touched starlight,
                        pale as rain
                    on her neck.
She took me
in the moonbow
                    of her arms.

I kissed
the jade
                    tiger-fire
            of her eyes.

60

A man woke to find his face
                    on a gold doubloon,
            & then it was his no more,

but was exchanged
                    in a white-water river
                                    of dream & contempt,
each person who touched it
                              changed
by the long trail
            of barterings
& dissemblings,
                                      palterings
                  & misgivings.

            To get what it must
was the first & foremost urge
                  of woodchuck
                            & woodpecker
      & of the toad
                with the brilliantly elastic tongue,
rolled up in its mouth
                  like a window blind.

            The snail,
                          the quail,
the town's thousand feral cats:
                each a guileless opportunist,
not one with an ounce
                            of human subterfuge,
            not one with a shred of human obliquity.

            Everyone knew the man's
                        stolen face
but no one knew him.
                & when he begged them
                      to return his face,
        they bruised his chest
                & broke his hands.

            Other people went to work
                      & got married
               & had children,
            & pursued their ever-
retreating dreams,
                admitting,
                      in moments of quiet clarity,
         their grand goals were becoming
                        thinner,
           more transparent,

more improbable
        & unlikely.

       His life was fixed
            & unchanging.
       Soon no one remembered him.

       Yet everyone wanted
the coin bearing his face.
       When friends gathered,
            they told stories of it.
       When lovers met,
         they saw its gleaming silver face.
       Children
dreamt of it.
       Old men & women
             spoke of it
        with their dying breaths.
       It inspired poets
           & mathematicians,
homeless printers
        & magicians.
       Inmates held it in their hearts
during their long ordeal
           of crime & time,
     & parents passed it
         without thinking
      to their children.

       One night
the man dreamed
           the most incredible
     & extravagant of dreams:
        His face came back to him.
       He could feel it
& see it in the mirror.
       When he woke,
         the rest of the world
       could not see him at all.
       He had completely
ceased to exist
       among them.

61

       Down silicate dunes,

across impossible dreams
                              of black glass & red clay,
the horsemen rode—
                    seven,
                            implacable,
                                        aloof,
                                commanding.
                Their horses' hooves,
ringed in steel,
                                    rang clean on stone,
                    sang of missed days
                        & forlorn nights,
of the broken chances
                                that always spell a desolation
                        of wants.

                The night's hair was braided
with weeping.
                The day's winding cloth
                                was woven of weeping.

                Factories spilled their workers' preserved hearts,
their pickled spirits,
                        the green maw
                            of determined & interminable desire.
                Smokestacks choked the sleek winds,
wrapped wire scarves
                                    round their slim necks
                        & squeezed
until the air became still
                                        as desert rock,
                    until storm sewers
                        thrust up a torrent of dead dogs.

                Weeping filled the air
with the cold taste
                                    of remorse.
                Weeping filled the air
                                    with the smoke
                    of unseen fires.

                The horsemen rode
                                into a mountain village.
                The air was thin
& the horses
                        were breathing hard.

The men dismounted
& drank cups full of spiders
                                    & delicate webs
             from the abandoned well.
Their horses slurped scorpions
from a dry trough.
The men eyed the sun
                   that hung at the meridian,
    a desiccated bread crust,
          a rough quartz icon.

That morning
             only mourning doves sang,
      weeping.
That evening
only bats & owls prayed,
                weeping.

Orphans trailed
             through the immolated streets.
Beggars collapsed
into dust & rotted teeth.
All the houses were littered
with dying mice.
The houseflies wriggled
                 eyelash-thin feet
      in slow but resolute death.

Yet empty clothes still got up
& went to work,
      & empty clothes
         still deposited their checks
    in the bank.
Weeping filled the plates
with coal grit & ash.
Weeping filled the pantry
          with steel filings
      & sand.

The horsemen
could not make their horses
             stand up.
They sent their last bullets
through the windows
    of the horses' skulls,
      watched them bleed

ball bearings
& toothless gear wheels
& miles of rust.

There was no shade
so the horsemen collapsed
against a compound's fence,
topped with razor wire.
As sun flamed to earth,
they gagged on their tongues.

Nothing was heard for a long time,
not even weeping.
Nothing was heard for a long time,
not even weeping.

62

The whole town fell asleep
& did not wake for days.
& when the people awoke,
they went around
asking each other about their dreams.

Do you remember?
Her face was a bowl of lemons.

Where are the black dogs?
There were hundreds
of black dogs.

& the whole sky
turned to numbers.
Each star
was a maze of equations.

Did you see the trees
become green bears
& fish salmon from the rivers?

For a whole day,
the rain flew up in torrents
from the earth.
& afterwards,
lakes floated darkly
above the new deserts.

But the more they learned,
the less they knew,

                              & they became sullen
& confused.
They vowed never to sleep again.

They were guarded,

                              nervous,
& quick to suspect their neighbors.
All night they walked in circles
on their hands,

                              so as not to doze off.
All day they cut nicks
on their arms & legs.

It wasn't sleep they feared

                              but dreams.

They made dreaming illegal
& speaking of dreams

                              & writing them down
& making songs of them
             & filming them
& choreographing ballets
& composing plays of them.

They no longer touched each other

                              in tenderness or desire.
Their tongues grew used
to silence,

                         their eyes to permanent vigilance.
They did not know
how long they could last.

They didn't realize they were awake

                            when they dreamed,
& were now asleep.
I was waiting
for the first of them

                              to awaken.

63

I would have called

                              on the dead angels—
I had so many questions—

                    but they left no footprints
          in the muddy street,
dropped no feather
                    like a passing dove or gull.
          I might have asked forgiveness,
but they had no interest in the past
                              or in anything bound
          & ruled by time.
          They cared nothing
for the ocean waves
                    that destroyed themselves
                              on the rocks,
          or the winds that had lost
                    their sense of direction,
or even for the frozen candelabras
                              of the amethyst stars.
          I'd built my life on questions,
                    but the dead appeared
                              to lack passion
          for both questions & answers.
          I acquiesced & kept my silence.

64

          The angels of the dispossessed
sang like radio atrophy
                    in the mind of the Bengal tiger
          of corporate malfeasance.
          The angels of the famished
sang like termites
                    sawing hardwood trees
                              with jaws like belts
          of machine gun bullets.

          The angels of the threadbare
sang like the waves of lakes,
                    burning skin from the bodies
          of children & other swimmers.

          The angels of the destitute
                    sang like a line of stones
in the cemeteries of health clubs
                    where nothing was healthy
          but the stock portfolios of board members.

65

The angels of the distressed
sang like icebergs calving in the sheets
                              of those who married
            as part of their relentless quest
                        for personal advantage in all things.

            The angels of the ruined
sang like the well-appointed
                                          & pampered,
                        craven as they whined & cried
about their loss of privilege
                        & market dominance,
                        which was the way they viewed
            every social interaction.

            The angels of the beggared
                                    sang like random satellites
broadcasting the news
                                    of the imminent fall
            of shopping malls,
                        meant as a balm & relief
                                    from the suffering resulting
from the perpetual perturbation
                        of the impulse to acquire.

            The angels of the forsaken
sang of the battery death
                        of automobiles & their abrupt slide
                                          into the stillness
                        & silence,
            unechoing & vast,
                        that refused to grant them quarter.

66

            I walked all the time in darkness now,
      bathed in
                  & warmed by
                              that enchantment of light
            that was not light
                        but what light might have been
                        had it been created for spirit or ear
& not air & the array
                  of ever-varying forms.

67

Daylight's lion sniffed
I as I lay on the ground.
She was curious.
I held my breath,
afraid of those massive paws,
those big-toothed jaws.
She padded into the tree line
& some other life
that was not that life.

68

Reading from halfway
around the planet
of the unrelenting bloodletting,
I understood:
I was that five year old,
hiding in the rubble of his home,
watching his mother be raped.
The boy had already watched them
cut down his father
& older brother
& mutilate their bodies.

He rushed out.
They shot him,
sprayed his blood
across a broken wall.
What would happen
in a future that came from
a past no one would claim?

69

Stragglers in the dark
moved warily past,
holding their breath
& looking down.
The only decisions
anyone felt free to make
were desecrations,
& no one wanted to be the first
to decide.
The alleyways grew darker,
& backyards were blank spaces
in the collective memory.

Not even feral cats felt safe.

Everywhere I heard the shouts
                              of the incensed,
the keening of those who'd learned
                        the pain of surviving
          those they loved most.

70

Humans believed they owned the earth,
& people expended their lives
                                trying to seize more
              & still more.
They defended their plots
with their blood,
            hoping to pass them down
                              to their children
          & their children's children.
But the earth was a vast grave,
& what the children inherited
                                was a grave.
          Why did no one demand
                        different choices?

71

Somewhere in the sable night of my grief,
a magenta pinhole opened
                  & grew golden,
                        until a green dragonfly
            squeezed through
& streaked on sheer wings,
                        speeding with bright beams
          through all the rooms.

Somewhere sable night
became golden,
              bright beams squeezed
                            through a green pinhole
          & sped on sheer wings
            through the magenta room
                              of my grief.

Somewhere grief became
a golden dragonfly,

        sped through a bright pinhole,
                 & streaked
    on night's green wings
        through the rooms' sable beams.

      Somewhere a golden room
grew green
        & a black dragonfly
          squeezed through magenta beams,
    streaked through a sheer pinhole,
        & sped on grief's bright wings
through sable night,
        somewhere in my house of song.

72

      Every night I dreamed of ocean.

      The moon drugged the sea
with its milky light,
        & all of the fish
               were enspelled.
      Sharks left off eating.

      Dolphins rested on wave crests,
dreaming.
      The water was sleek
               & sick
        with warm opaline light.

      As gulls drowned
& turtles sank,
             giant squid stretched tentacles
        toward unknown depths.

      Meteors sizzled like lucifers
dropped into water,
        & the earth drifted,
             drifted,
    inert as the victim
        of some random beating.

      I thought I'd known grief.
      I'd known nothing.

73

The ocean was bedazzled
by alabaster light.
              The shattered ship
                        descended into the blacker waters
      below,
              a nothing
                                swallowed
                        by a vaster nothing.

              I lay suspended
on the cold & pallid waves,
                        spared but unforgiven,
                                        forsaken.
              I waited,
waited for the preposterous,
                                the impossible—
                  for the dawn to break
      & the ship of some mercy
                        to appear
              & bear toward me.

74

              Every night I dreamed of ocean.

              We chose not to leave
the dream of the sea.

              Immortal jellies floated,
                  transparent as windows,
                              in the water,
& the sun died into
                        & was resurrected
        from the unceasing waves.
              Had we found the crimson wreck
of barriers
                  & barricades
                              of encrusted coral,
      water-
              born phantasmagoria
                              & abstruse flowerings,
                  perishable,
              ingenious
                        water queendoms,
deft & sumptuous

sanctuaries
of stationary flight,
of flaming dark,
fluorescing in the leafy lobes
of seadragons at swim,
a dangerous feast
of beasts & words,
restive, resounding,
& rare?
It is largely uncharted
but still likely related
to the archaic clarity,
the charity
of undying eel grass
& the great white sharks
of imagination's
dead reckoning,
& of lush temples
& theaters & wraiths.
Does music trace
the flight of garrulous gulls?
Light the blue whales'
starless chambers?
Love seeks perpetual day
or perpetual night.
Time,
to no one's surprise,
refuses to comply.
Love is willing to drown
to learn how to swim.

75

Walking a steep path,
I heard these words:
Climb from the jaguar's forest
to the Inca's house.
Walk through the trapezoidal door
into time
& slavery
& execution.
& as you work
in the midnight graves
of the silver mines,
hold fast to your desire
to drink,

like the condor,
        the air between mountain peaks,
    to walk sure-footed
        as a llama
          up the rocks.

Choose the green fire
of mountain air
    in your lungs,
      choose the truth
        like an obsidian blade
      in your chest.
The mines have—
      & will always have—
new masters.
    Only words
      can smash
        your manacles.
    Only words
can make you
      masterless.

Take this path
      all the way to Tierra del Fuego.
Clouds show the way.
Kind words are your passport,
though no one trusts them.
So be prepared
      to steal across borders.

You may never return,
but you knew that
      when you started.

76

    Radioactive coral,
pearl sprung from the shoulder
      of midnight's chancery.
    The square root of air
        is coal,
    a star of ice,
a million mutations
    of the possible.

The indistinct river

                    becomes distinct
& the eye's torpedo
                        explodes
     the random number generator.

      Night after night my ghosts drink
from the goblet of rancor
                 & razorblades,
       of repentance & regret,
    in a room frosted
           with cold moonlight.
     I can't breathe in the helium
of my distance.
     As tenderness drains like blood
            from my face,
    disappointment flows in
       to replace it.

77

     A ceibo,
red as arterial blood,
            turns brown & dies.
     A ruffled blue sheaf
       of feathers,
the swallow-tailed manakin
         stares hard
          into day's first light
    as a voice speaks
       from the battlements of air.
    Are you the person,
hapless
      & hopeless,
         blown out of a plane
       blown out of the sky,
the geographer of a mute certainty,
        the will of a catapult?
    If so,
         you are one I seek,
      & it is fortune itself
that has brought you
       to me through this infinite labyrinth.

     I wanted to answer,
but the voice was gone.
     The speech joined hundreds of others

                        in the museum
              of unfinished conversations.

78

              The midnight bead
brought my beloved to me.
              We talked until she fell asleep,
                        her head on the moon's hand.

              My breath became braided
                        in her hair
& my eyes stroked
              her cheeks & neck.
              As my fingers traced her arm's
warm cinnamon,
                        I kissed the line on her throat
              between shadow & light,
kissed her temples,
              where larks secreted themselves,
       kissed her forehead,
              where dreams played out,
                        disembodied
              as the light at the ruby's heart.

              Singing her name,
syllables soft
              as eyelashes on cheeks,
                        I lay down beside her
       to sleep,
              my head on the moon's other hand.

79

              Rain hauled up the tall mainsails
                        of the forest
& forced the grass'
              soft follicles.

              Dead comrades
                        lay still under the canopies.
              The great Chilean poet
sang what they could not.

              In the wet season,
                        the moon drank

            until its belly bulged,
until it became sodden
         & denuded of desire.
    The rising sun scuttled
             a fleet of clouds.

    He dived deep into the sea
& leaped up again in flames.

    Beneath the planet's green skin,
its fertile black shell,
     & beneath the mountains,
          great flat slabs
     & porous shelves,
needle spikes
     & blunt bluffs & boulders—
         all chanted
   a single continuous tone,
     deeper than any gong or bell.

    In the earth,
the dead heard it,
    & they opened
        their cold bony mouths
    to intone it, too.

    From the old stones,
         he learned to sing
in the key of the dead,
     that he might solace the living.

80

    I wore out a pair of shoes
before I reached
     the rock-strewn shore
         of southern Argentina
   & stood,
     at the very end of day,
like Balboa gazing,
    rapt,
        at the vast expanse
    of the Pacific.
   I stared straight across
the Strait of Magellan
     at the distant broken-

boned islands
of Tierra del Fuego.

I faced serious water
for the first time.
The ocean was far more imposing
& imperial,
more restless
& relentless,
than the lakes I had swum,
the innumerable creeks
I had splashed across,
or the rivers I had forded.

There,
on the last rocky outpost
of the landmass,
the sea winds strove
to topple me
from my perch
into the waves,
as they smashed
against the continent
& sprayed up,
in splendid,
exquisite futility,
toward the millions
of emerging stars.

An orca breached
& swam toward me.
I felt summoned,
commanded to walk out
onto the moon's wide white wake.
My blood flamed in answer,
& even if it were to plunge
to my death,
I must obey.

I stepped off the boulder,
ready for the drop,
the frozen submersion.
Instead,
I stepped onto the orca's back.

It turned

& churned

through the choppy water,
& I strove to stay upright.

We were soon in ocean

deeper
than any of my dreams.

Water spray
sheathed my clothes & hair

in ice.
Only some pure fire within

kept me from freezing.

The orca swam faster.
It never tired,
though I thought I would expire

from exhaustion.

Just when I knew
I could no longer stand
& began the slow,

inexorable fall
into turbulent black water,

we arrived,
the orca stopped,
&,

impelled by our motion,
I flew onto the vast snow-
&-ice-covered land.

My blood blazed
& I struggled to my feet.
I looked out to sea,

but the orca was gone.
In a trance,
I turned
& began to trek

to the interior.

I didn't know how many days it was
before I arrived at the Station,
but when I did,

she was there—
my beloved,
my wife,

loyal beyond my lunacy.

& there,
in the land
where the air was so cold
it didn't rain
& almost never snowed,
where most of the world's fresh water
lay locked in a block
as big as a large country,
there love set aflame
the body that had dwelled
in peril
& nearly perished.

I felt hot as the summer day
I'd started my long walk.

& I felt peace.

81

A song's lament
surprised
like coconut milk
on her lips.
Let me drink it again.
I hung the moon,
a feather,
in her hair,
& we were rose quartz
& moonstone.

Give me that guitar,
lush as bougainvillea,
weeping arterial light
into day.

The song wreathed us like smoke,
slid like smoke between.
It touched her shoulders
& the midnight roses
of her hair.
The song spiraled down long legs,
spilled down arms.

We spoke
             & dark nebulae
                      floated between us,
a swirling syllable dance.
          Lips found lips
                 & words became kisses,
       flaming strings of prominences,
                  solar winds.
         Hands searched
& we touched
                 in a silver landscape
           of memory & requital.

         The song poured from me
into her
                 & back into me.
         We let the guitarist's
gracile fingers
            trill staccato fire
                 up spines.
         Skin flushed with song,
flesh sang with beat
            & blood.

         We let that guitar
            play through me,
                 through her,
through endless night
           & waking.

         Sidereal furnaces
consumed planets
          & moons
                 & desire's corona
           burned beyond flame,
      until we reached the final,
             infinite,
               tender
collapse within,
         to ineffable density,
               a gravity so great
      nothing but these words
           could escape.

Notes

The Whitman epigraph is from "Song of Myself."

Sections 55-57 takes as their subject the acts of femicide that have occurred in Ciudad Juárez over the past several decades. The murders number in the hundreds.

Section 62 is in conversation with the insomnia plague chapter of Gabriel García Márquez's *One Hundred Years of Solitude.*

Sections 63, 64, & 65 pay homage to Rafael Alberti's *Concerning the Angels.*

Section 74 is in conversation with Cat Dixon's "My lover has left, and everything is worse now." The immortal jellyfish, or Turritopsis dohrnii, is at least theoretically able to elude death. For more information, see https://oceanconservancy.org/blog/2019/07/01/immortal-jellyfish-lives-name.

The poet referenced in section 79 is Pablo Neruda. The allusion in the last stanza is to section XII of "The Heights of Macchu Picchu," specifically the line, "I come to speak through your dead mouth," translated by Mariela Griffor.

Acknowledgments

I am grateful to the editors of these magazines & presses, in whose pages versions of these poems appeared, sometimes under different titles:
Cathexis Northwest Press: Sections 63-71; section 74 (nominated for a Pushcart Prize)

Evergreen Review: Sections 58 & 61

The Good Life Review: Section 60 (nominated for Best of the Net)

Passager: Section 39

Peacock Journal: Sections 34, 35, 36, 41, 54, 76, & 77 (the last two appeared as a single poem and were reprinted in the *Peacock Journal* quarterly anthology)

The West Review: Section 48

A version of section 2, appeared in the anthology, *Filling the Empty Room.*

A different version of parts I & III of *As Jaguars Dreamed on the Earth's Dark Face* appeared as a chapbook titled *The Book of Night & Waking.* It was selected by John Sibley Williams as the 2019 winner of the Cathexis Northwest Press Chapbook Prize. *As Jaguars Dreamed on the Earth's Dark Face* is more than triple the length of the chapbook and has an entirely new lineation. Numerous additions have been made, including the whole of Part II.

Versions of sections 34, 35, 36, 41, 54, 72, 73, 76, & 77 appeared, without titles, in the chapbook, *Self-Portraits in Which I Do Not Appear* (Finishing Line Press).

I extend my deepest gratitude and thanks to C. M. Tollefson, for believing in this book and for shepherding it with such loving care, such a brilliant eye, and such skilled hands into the world. He is the publishing partner and collaborator every writer should have.

A Pushcart and Best of the Net nominee, Clif Mason lives with his wife, a visual artist, on the edge of a forest in Bellevue, Nebraska. He is the author of KNOCKING THE STARS SENSELESS (Stephen F. Austin State University Press), and three chapbooks: THE BOOK OF NIGHT & WAKING (winner of the Cathexis Northwest Press Chapbook Prize), SELF-PORTRAITS IN WHICH I DO NOT APPEAR (Finishing Line Press), and FROM THE DEAD BEFORE (Lone Willow Press). His work has appeared in *Rattle, Southern Poetry Review, The Classical Outlook, Evergreen Review, Poet Lore, Iota* (UK) and *Orbis International Literary Journal* (UK), among many others. His poems have been featured at and/or awarded prizes by the Joe Gouveia Outermost Poetry Contest (selected by Marge Piercy as First Place in the National Category & Grand Prize winner), Negative Capability Press, Cathexis Northwest Press, *Plainsongs, Writers' Journal, SPSM&H, Amelia*, the Midwest Writers' Conference, and the Academy of American Poets. He is a former Fulbright Fellow to Rwanda, Africa.

Also Available
from
Cathexis Northwest Press:

Something To Cry About
by Robert Krantz

Suburban Hermeneutics
by Ian Cappelli

God's Love Is Very Busy
by David Seung

that one time we were almost people
by Christian Czaniecki

Fever Dream/Take Heart
by Valyntina Grenier

The Book of Night & Waking
by Clif Mason

Dead Birds of New Zealand
by Christian Czaniecki

The Weathering of Igneous Rockforms in High-Altitude Riparian Environments
by John Belk

If A Fish
by George Burns

How to Draw a Blank
by Collin Van Son

En Route
by Jesse Wolfe

sky bright psalms
by Temple Cone

Moonbird
by Henry G. Stanton

southern athiest. oh, honey
by d. e. fulford

Bruises, Birthmarks & Other Calamities
by Nadine Klassen

Wanted: Comedy, Addicts
by AR Dugan

They Curve Like Snakes
by David Alexander McFarland

the catalog of daily fears
by Beth Dufford

Shops Close Too Early
by Josh Feit

Vanity Unfair and Other Poems
by Robert Eugene Rubino

Destructive Heresies
by Milo E. Gorgevska

Cathexis Northwest Press